W9-BQY-670

by BERNARD WABER

Lyle and the Birthday Party

Houghton Mifflin Company, Boston

for Kim Louisa

All rights reserved. For information about permission
to reproduce selections from this book, write to
Permissions, Houghton Mifflin Company, 215 Park Avenue
South, New York, New York 10003.

Printed in the United States of America

Library of Congress Card Catalog Number: AC66-10406

ISBN 0-395-17451-1 (pbk.)   ISBN 0-395-15080-9 (rnf.)

WOZ   30 29 28 27 26 25 24 23

It was Joshua's birthday.
The Primms were happily busy
with party preparations. Lyle the
Crocodile who lived with
them was busy, too.

And as usual, Lyle was being helpful.
Parties were fun. He wished he
could have one. He'd have colorful
streamers, just like these . . .

and balloons as big as this . . .

and a cake, exactly the size Mrs. Primm
was decorating for Joshua,
he told himself.

The more Lyle thought about it,
the more he too wanted a
birthday party.
"Why shouldn't I have a birthday party?"
he asked himself. "I was born, wasn't I?"

Suddenly, like storm clouds coming down
upon a lovely day, Lyle was jealous;
mean green jealous of Joshua's soon-
to-be-celebrated birthday party.

Lyle didn't want to be jealous. It felt
awful, in fact. Besides, he loved Joshua
dearly. But the more he smiled and tried to
cover up, the more jealous he seemed to become.
Worse still, Lyle was sure everyone could
read his unhappy thoughts.

Lyle almost forgot about being jealous
when the party guests arrived.

He even told himself he was having a
marvelous time. He played musical chairs . . .

pin-the-tail . . .

and gave each of the winners
a turn on his back.

But when it came time for Joshua to blow out the candles, the mean, jealous feelings began to return. Lyle could just picture himself blowing.

And it was more than he could bear
to watch Joshua unwrap his gifts.
Oh, how Lyle wished they were his
to unwrap!

By the time the party was over, Lyle was in
a dark, dreadful mood. He hardly recognized
himself. While Joshua thanked his guests for
coming, Lyle just stood by sulking and scarcely
even waved goodbye.
Everyone was so surprised.
This wasn't a bit like the Lyle
they knew and loved.

To make matters worse, that very night
Lyle stepped right through a toy drum,
a favorite birthday gift of Joshua's.
Everyone said it was an accident and
Lyle shouldn't feel bad about it.

But was it an accident?
Lyle went to bed not feeling
at all sure.

The next day at breakfast, the Primms
were still talking about the party.
"Whatever can be keeping Lyle?" Mrs. Primm
suddenly asked. "His breakfast will
be getting ice-cold."

Mrs. Primm called up to him.
"Lyle! Lyle! Breakfast!"
A very sad Lyle, feeling a full measure
of shame for his behavior the day before,
made his way down the stairs.
"Something is wrong with Lyle,"
said Mrs. Primm.

"He seems all right to me," said Mr. Primm.
"He isn't smiling," said Mrs. Primm.
"Perhaps he doesn't feel like smiling,"
Mr. Primm replied. "After all, he's only . . ."
Mr. Primm caught himself about to say "human."
"Nevertheless," said Mrs. Primm,
"I do believe he's coming down with something.
Now let me think," she said. "What has been
going around? Chicken pox? Mumps? Measles?
Oh dear!" she exclaimed. "There have been several
cases of measles in the neighborhood."
"I doubt seriously that Lyle has measles or anything
else for that matter," Mr. Primm
broke in, rather sharply.

"All the same," said Mrs. Primm, "I'll just have
a look at his throat. There," she said,
"just as I suspected. It's pink and scratchy-looking."
"It's always pink and scratchy-looking," said
Mr. Primm. "Besides, it wouldn't surprise me if
a good, hearty breakfast cures whatever is
ailing Lyle."

Everyone returned to the table.
But Lyle only picked at his food
and didn't seem at all hungry.

"There, did you see?" said Mrs. Primm.
"He didn't touch a speck of food;
not one speck."
Mr. Primm was off to work and Joshua to school.
"Now, now," said Mr. Primm, "Lyle is
going to be all right. I'm quite sure of it."

But Lyle wasn't all right. He moped about the entire morning. He didn't seem to want to go out. He didn't seem to want to do his chores. He really didn't seem to want to do anything.

Mrs. Primm wondered if she should call a doctor;
but whom to call? Certainly not her family doctor;
what would he know about crocodiles? What about the zoo?
"Now that was being sensible," she told herself.
Surely someone there would know how to advise her.

"Please," said Mrs. Primm, when she was connected with the zoo, "my crocodile isn't feeling well today. Could you kindly recommend a good crocodile doctor?"

"Where is this crocodile?" a man asked.

"He's right beside me, here in the living room," said Mrs. Primm.

"Living room?"

"Yes," said Mrs. Primm.

"You did say living room?" the man made sure.

"Yes . . . LIV . . . ING ROOOOM. Please," continued Mrs. Primm, "he must have a doctor."

"Well . . ." The man hesitated.

"Yes, do go on," pressed Mrs. Primm.

"Well, there is a Dr. Lewis James on East 65th Street who is very good with crocodiles."

"Dr. Lewis James. Oh thank you. Thank you so very much," said Mrs. Primm gratefully.

The instant Mrs. Primm put down the receiver, she
realized she had forgotten to ask for the doctor's tele-
phone number. She wondered if she should call the
zoo again and decided she wouldn't.
"No problem really," she cheered herself on.
"His name is DR. LEWIS JAMES and . . ." Mrs. Primm stopped.
Had she caught the name correctly? Was it DR. LEWIS JAMES?
Or was it . . . could it possibly have been . . . DR. JAMES LEWIS?
"Whatever is wrong with me this morning?" she asked herself.
"Lewis James, James Lewis, Lewis James, James Lewis,"
she recited over and over, trying to fit the two names
like stubborn pieces in a jigsaw puzzle.
"DR. JAMES LEWIS rather does sound more like it,"
she finally persuaded herself.

"Hello, operator." Mrs. Primm was on the
telephone again. "Would you please tell me if
there is a Dr. James Lewis located on East 65th Street."
"Yes, there is," answered the operator, after a moment.
"Would you like to be connected with him?"
"Oh thank you; please, yes," said Mrs. Primm.
"There, I was right." She sighed with great relief.
But Mrs. Primm wasn't right. In fact, she couldn't
have been more sadly wrong.
The Dr. James Lewis she was about to speak with,
although an excellent doctor for children, knew precious
little about the condition of crocodiles.

"Doctor," said Mrs. Primm when she was connected,
"my crocodile isn't feeling well today."
Dr. Lewis was sure he had heard the word "crocodile";
in fact, he was quite sure. But then, the good doctor
was accustomed to excited callers.
"Who did you say wasn't feeling well?" he asked with
his usual comforting, bedside voice.
"Lyle," answered Mrs. Primm
"Lyle . . . I see," said the doctor. "Now tell me, how old is Lyle?'
"I really can't be sure," said Mrs. Primm. "You see, we
found him here when we moved in."
"You found him! How extraordinary!" exclaimed the doctor.
Dr. Lewis took a necessary few seconds to collect himself
before going on to his next question.
"Does he have a temperature?" he asked.
"I don't know," said Mrs. Primm.
"Well . . . does he appear flushed?"
"I can't be sure of that either," she answered.
"He's so green, you know."
"His face is green?" asked the doctor.
"Why he's green all over," said Mrs. Primm.
"Madam!" the doctor gasped. "This sounds like an
emergency. Wrap him warmly and put him to bed. I'll
have an ambulance come fetch him at once."

Mrs. Primm got Lyle to bed as the doctor ordered.
Shortly after, the ambulance was at her door.

The ambulance attendants looked in astonishment
at the great, green figure stretched out on the bed.
Next, they looked at each other.
"What do you think?" whispered one.
"I don't know. What do you think?" whispered the other.
"Is your name Mrs. Primm?" they asked.
"Yes."
"Is the patient's name Lyle?"
"Yes."
"Is this East 88th Street?"
"Of course," Mrs. Primm replied with growing impatience.
"What's wrong with him?" they wanted to know.
"I just don't know," said Mrs. Primm, in tears now.
"There, there," said the attendants, "now don't you
worry, lady. He's going to be all right."

"Maybe it's one of those rare illnesses," whispered
one attendant as they lowered Lyle down the stairs.
" 'Crocodilitis,' for instance."
"If that's what it is, this one sure has a bad case of
it," whispered the other.
"Now do be careful of his tail, please," Mrs. Primm
called down from the top of the stairs.
"We will, lady," they answered.

"I must not be feeling too well myself today,"
thought the lady in the hospital office when Lyle
and Mrs. Primm were brought to her. She tried not to
stare at the new patient. "It's not polite to stare,"
she reminded herself and quickly got busy with questions.
"Patient's name please?" said the lady.
"Lyle," answered Mrs. Primm looking around.
Something was wrong. This hardly seemed a proper
hospital for crocodiles.
"Lyle what?" the lady wanted to know.
Mrs. Primm grew even more suspicious.
"Just Lyle," she answered.
"He doesn't have a last name?"
"Last name?" Mrs. Primm repeated.
Now she was sure a dreadful mistake had been made.
"Well, how are you related?" asked the lady.
"Please," said Mrs. Primm, when she had found her voice.
"I'm sure Lyle wasn't meant to come here. I'll take
him home at once."
"Take him home?" said the lady. "But you can't
take him home; not without his doctor's permission.
Rules are rules, you know!" she exclaimed.

So it was that Lyle became a patient.
He was dressed in a hospital gown . . .

and put to bed.

"Good morning," said his nurse, the following day.
"Time to freshen up." It was still dark outside.
Lyle hated to wake up.
"Come along, lazybones," said the nurse.

"My what large teeth you have,"
the nurse remarked.

"Ah, ah, ah, mustn't bite
the thermometer."

After breakfast, Lyle was too restless to go
back to sleep. Besides, he was curious about
this big, strange place that was the hospital.

Although they were surprised to see him,
the other patients took to Lyle immediately.
"Please," said one, "would you raise my head
so that I may read?" Lyle was glad to be of service.

"Please," said another,
"would you lower my shade?"

Lyle spent the rest of the morning
pouring glasses of water . . .

changing television programs . . .

and giving aid
wherever it was wanted.

When he discovered where they were,
he particularly enjoyed amusing the children.
"More, more," they called as Lyle danced, leaped,
did handstands, headstands, and somersaulted about.   43

To his, theirs, and everyone's great surprise,
Lyle's last and best somersault landed him
kerplunk directly at the feet of Mrs. Primm, Dr. Lewis,
and the nurse; the three of whom had been frantically
searching for him. The nurse scolded Lyle
for being out of bed.
"Lyle," she said, "you are supposed to be sick. Remember?"
Lyle smiled. He wasn't feeling a bit sick. Doing for
others had made him feel good again; so good in fact,
he completely forgot about being jealous.

"So this is the famous Lyle I have been hearing so much about,"
said the doctor. "I would say his health seems most improved.
Don't you agree, Mrs. Primm?"

Mrs. Primm agreed.

"In fact," the doctor went on, "I would say Lyle appears
well enough to go home today."

"Doctor, I am so sorry for the trouble . . ." Mrs. Primm
began to apologize.

"Don't be sorry," the doctor interrupted. "It seems to me
Lyle is the best medicine our patients have had
in a good, long time."

Lyle made many friends during his short stay
at the hospital. "Goodbye," they called out.
"Come back again."
"But only for a visit, mind you," Dr. Lewis
added with a somewhat nervous chuckle.

Several days later, returning from a shopping trip,
Mrs. Primm had something important to tell Lyle.
"Lyle," she said, "did you know there was
something very special about today?"
Lyle didn't know.
"Well," said Mrs. Primm, "today marks an anniversary —
exactly three years since we found you. And . . ."

SURPRISE! There was going to be a party to celebrate.
Lyle's party.